Somebody is hiding in the old Ghost
Hotel. Is it just some homeless guy?
Or is it a real ghost?
Kyle and Josh are willing to risk
their necks to find out.

GHOST HOTEL

Paul Kropp

HIP·JR.

HIP Junior

LIBRARY AND ARCHIVES CANADA CATALOGUING IN PUBLICATION

Kropp, Paul
  Ghost hotel / Paul Kropp.

(HIP jr)
ISBN 978-1-897039-98-4

  I. Title. II. Series: HIP jr

PS8571.R772G45 2010   jC813'.54   C2010-904379-0

General editor: Paul Kropp
Text design and typesetting: Laura Brady
Illustrations drawn by: Charlie Hnatiuk
Cover design: Robert Corrigan

2 3 4   20 19 18

Printed and bound in Canada

Canada

High Interest Publishing acknowledges the financial support of the
Government of Canada through the Canada Book Fund for its
publishing activities.

CHAPTER 1

Worries

Our mom worries too much. She worries about us riding our bikes on the street. She worries about how lousy we do at school. She worries about us playing at the old hotel just behind our house.

"If I catch you boys playing near the hotel, I'm going to smack you both," Mom says.

"Mom, you never smack us," I told her. And that's the truth. Though she once grounded me for two weeks.

Then she says, "Kyle, don't talk back."

Mostly, I don't talk back. But my little brother, Josh, does. He's only eight years old so he can get away with it.

Josh and I live on the edge of a small town called Dansville. Just behind our house, up the hill, is a big, old hotel. The hotel was built over a hundred years ago. Back then, lots of people took the railroad to come stay there. The hotel was like a spa. It was supposed to have "healing waters" that made sick people feel better. Maybe it did. But then the "healing waters" dried up. The railroad stopped running. And the hotel closed its doors long before my mom was born.

So now we have a big, boarded-up hotel, with no roof and no windows, just behind our house. Maybe that's why our rent is so cheap.

"Do you think there are ghosts up in the hotel?" Josh asked me.

"Josh, you're an idiot," I said.

Josh gave me one of those looks. "Mom," Josh yelled out. "Kyle called me an idiot."

My mother appeared at the door. "Kyle Reynolds! If you call your brother an idiot one more time, I'm going to ground you for a month." I had heard that one before. "Now tell Josh you're sorry."

"I'm sorry, Josh," I said in a sing-song voice. But I had my fingers crossed.

"That's good," our mother said. "Now you two play together while I go to the store. No fights. If I catch you fighting …"

I groaned.

As soon as Mom got the car out of the driveway, Josh was back at it.

"So are there ghosts?" he asked me. "Up there. At the hotel?"

"There's no such thing as ghosts," I told him.

"How do you know?" Josh asked. "What makes you think you're so smart, Kyle? Lots of people believe in ghosts. There's a girl in my class who's even *seen* a ghost."

"How old is this girl?"

"Eight."

"Just like you. So she's an idiot, just like you."

Josh was going to shout for Mom, but then he remembered she wasn't home.

"You shouldn't call me names," he muttered.

"I didn't call you a name," I explained. "I said that you and that girl were both idiots if you believe in ghosts. There's no such thing as ghosts. When people die, they die. The elements in the body break down and return to the earth." I learned that in my grade 7 science class.

"But what about God and angels and Heaven?"

"That's something else," I told him. "It's not ghosts. There are no ghosts in the Bible, or ghouls, or werewolves."

"But I saw lights," Josh said, "up in the hotel."

"When?"

"Last night. And the night before that," Josh told me. "The lights move around inside. It's like they go from room to room."

"It must be teenagers. They break in the place to party and get drunk," I told him.

"How do you know? It could be a ghost," Josh

shot back. "What makes you think you're so smart, anyhow?"

"Because I *am* smart," I told him. "And there's no such thing as ghosts."

That's when Josh got this funny look on his face. It was like he had a big smile inside that was about to turn into a belly laugh.

"So prove it," he said. "If you're so sure of yourself, you go inside the old hotel after dark. You look around and then tell me there's no ghosts."

"That's stupid," I told him.

"You're scared."

"Mom would get mad," I added.

"She doesn't have to know," Josh said. "And she's mad at us all the time anyhow." He waited a second and then came up with the clincher. "So if there are no ghosts, there's no reason to be scared, right?"

"I'm not scared," I said, cool as could be.

My brother shot me a look. "So prove it, Kyle. You go into the old hotel and I'll do all the dishes for a month. All of them. For a month – washing *and* drying. How's that for a deal?"

In our house, the dishwasher has been busted since Josh was born. So Josh and I have to wash and dry the dishes every night. I wash, Josh dries. But I *hate* washing dishes. Suddenly the deal was starting to sound good.

"What are you going to do when I go in there?" I asked him.

"I'm going to be right behind you," Josh said. "At least until we see the first ghost."

CHAPTER 2

Up the Stairs

We finished dinner and then went out to play. At least, that's what we told Mom. "We're going to play next door," we told her, and she grunted. We never play next door, but that didn't matter. It got us out of the house.

In no time we had climbed up to the hotel. It loomed over our heads, four storeys high. It must have had a hundred rooms in the old days. There were towers on each end, like a castle would have. In the center was a set of big windows, all boarded

over with plywood. Maybe they were windows to a lobby, or a ballroom. In front of us was a pair of big doors in an arch of carved stone. The stone was carved with animals and strange faces. The doors themselves were made of dark wood, but they were pretty messed up. The whole place had been on fire a couple of times, so the windows were all gone. But the old stone walls were still there, just like a hundred years ago.

"It looks scary," Josh said.

"It looks like a wreck," I told him. "It's not scary, just burned out."

"Maybe people died in the fire."

"And became ghosts?" I asked him.

"Yeah, maybe," Josh replied. He was still looking up at the hotel with an open mouth.

I just shook my head. Josh is only eight, but he's pretty stupid for a kid that age. I mean, it was only last year that he stopped believing in Santa Claus.

"C'mon," I said. "We're going in."

There were twenty steps up ahead of us. They

led to the main doors of the Ghost Hotel. And the doors were locked.

"What now?" Josh asked.

"We need a crowbar," I told him. "You sneak down to the house and get one from the shed."

"Why me?"

"Because you're little," I told him. "And you're sneaky."

"Is that good?"

"In this case, it is. Now go get me a crowbar ... real quick."

Josh took off back to the house. That left me alone in front of the old hotel – the Ghost Hotel. I just laughed. But the sun was going down behind the hill, and the bugs were coming out. I was more afraid of the bugs than any ghosts. It's the real world that's scary, not the stuff we make up.

A wind came up while I was waiting. I could hear something banging inside the house. *It's the wind*, I told myself. But I still jumped. The noise was kind of weird, and then there was this whistling sound. *It's the wind*, I repeated.

Josh came back about fifteen minutes later.

"What took you?"

"The crowbar wasn't there," Josh said. "So I brought a hammer."

"Oh, great," I told him. "Can't you do anything right?"

"Just try it," Josh said.

So I took the claw of the hammer and wedged it between one of the doors and the frame. A little push and the door popped open.

"See," Josh said proudly. "I told you a hammer would work."

The two of us walked inside. Ahead of us was a big, big room, three storeys high. It must have been a ballroom way back when. There were metal columns on each side and fancy staircases leading upstairs.

"Cool," Josh said.

"Sick!" I told him. The walls were stained with smoke and dirt. The plaster ceiling had crashed onto the floor. The metal columns were rusty and bent. The place was a wreck. "No ghost would hang around here."

"Ghosts don't care about dirt," Josh said. "They *like* dirt!"

I gave him a look. "How do you know?"

Josh didn't answer. Instead, he began walking into the ballroom. I had to tell him to be careful. There was no telling if he might fall right through the floor.

"Okay, so I win," I said. "There's no ghosts … so you do dishes for a month."

"There's no ghosts *here*," Josh said. "But the lights were upstairs."

I looked at the two staircases. They were both about to fall over. I tried one to see if I could shake the thing with my hand.

"I'm not risking my life on that," I told Josh.

"So look around," Josh replied. "There have to be some other stairs. I mean, this was a really big hotel."

Sometimes my stupid brother can be really smart. Off to the left, behind the ballroom, was a good set of stairs. In no time we were up on the second floor, and then the third.

That's when we heard it. A creak.

"What was that?" Josh asked.

"Shhh," I told him. "It's the wind," I whispered.

"No it's not," he whispered back to me. "It's …
something."

Then we heard it again. A creak. Then another.
Like slow footsteps over our heads.

"It's a ghost," Josh said. His voice was high and
scared.

"It's the wind," I told him. But it didn't sound
much like the wind. It sounded like somebody
walking. A person walking … I hoped.

"I'm scared," Josh said.

So was I, but I wasn't going to tell him that.
"Let's get out of here," I whispered.

"No," Josh said. "You promised."

"Promised what?"

"That there's no ghosts," he said. "So now you
have to go look. Or else you're a wuss. A liar and a
wuss."

Okay, so maybe my stupid brother is mostly
stupid. But I wasn't going to be a wuss. I wasn't

going to give up over a few strange noises.

So I slowly went up the last set of stairs – twelve of them – one at a time. I was about halfway up when my head got above the floor level. I could see another wrecked room. I could see sunshine coming through the wrecked roof. But that wasn't all I saw.

"Ohmygod!" I screamed. And then I froze.

CHAPTER 3

Meeting the Ghost

My brother pushed up beside me, and then he stared too. In front of us was a ghost, or what looked like a ghost. It was a man, dressed all in white. He had white skin and red hair and eyes that sunk into his face.

"Are you dead?" my brother asked.

The ghost turned and stared at us. His eyes seemed to glow red, like they were shooting a death ray.

"Dead?" replied the ghost. "Dead? Dead! Dead!!"

And then he started laughing like a crazy guy.

I couldn't breathe. I couldn't swallow. I couldn't do anything but stare at this … thing.

Then the ghost fell to the floor. He started crawling toward us, all the time with that crazy laugh.

I thought I was going to pee my pants. No, I *did* pee my pants.

I wanted to run. I wanted to get out of there as fast as any live person could move. But I couldn't. I was frozen.

But my brother kept walking up the stairs. Soon Josh was right up on the top floor, looking right at the ghost. For a second, I thought the ghost might grab my brother and … I don't know what. But that didn't happen.

Instead, my brother shot off his mouth. "You're no ghost!" he said. Josh sounded cheated, like he'd just gotten a broken toy as a prize at McDonald's.

"Ghost! Dead! Dead! Dead!" repeated the ghost. It was like a chant – the music of a madman.

"You've got bad breath," my brother said. "And

ghosts don't have any breath." My brother sounded really certain about this.

The ghost stopped crawling. He sat back on his heels, and then his face changed. He wasn't scary anymore, just kind of sad. For a second I thought he might cry.

"Don't I look like a ghost?" the ghost asked.

"No, you look like our science teacher at school," Josh told him. "Except you've got funny hair."

"It's perfectly good hair," the ghost said. "It's just red … and a little dirty. If you live in old buildings, you get a little dirty."

Suddenly I could breathe again. I could move. I could make my way up the stairs to stand beside my brother. It was like a magic spell had been broken.

"So who are you?" I asked the guy.

"You two may call me Dr. J, the peripatetic historian."

"Peripa … what?" Josh asked.

"Peripatetic," he replied. "It means 'travelling.' I

travel across the country, talking about history wherever I go. I am a historian of the streets. A teacher of the common man."

His eyes still looked a little crazy.

"Does that mean you don't have a job?" I asked.

Dr. J sighed. "A job? I have had many jobs, many positions. I have taught at great schools. Great colleges. I have books in many libraries. At this very moment, I have many job offers that I am considering."

"So you're a bum," Josh said. And then he laughed because he said the word *bum*.

"And you are cruel, young man," Dr. J lectured Josh. "Do not judge a man by the dirt in his hair or the clothes on his body. A man can only be judged by this!" he pointed at the side of his head.

"Your ears?" Josh asked.

Dr. J groaned. In just two minutes, he knew what I'd been going through for eight years.

"No, my mind!" Dr. J shouted. "My mind is full of knowledge. My mind is full of history – stories, facts, dates."

From his looks, I figured his mind was full of garbage. So I decided to check. "Okay, so what's the history of this place?"

"Ah, a young man looking for truth," Dr. J replied, looking at me.

"Yeah, so?"

"So this building is on the site of Dansville Water Cures, built in 1858. That first building was made entirely of wood … and it burned to the ground in 1882. To make sure that could not happen again, this building was made of iron and stone. It became Dr. Jackson's Sanatorium."

"What's a sanatorium?" Josh asked.

Dr. J smiled. "From the Latin *sana* for "health" and *torium* for "place." This place restored the health of thousands of people. Men and women would take the train from New York just to come here." He pointed around at the burned-out room. "Dr. Jackson taught people to exercise – boxing, swimming, dancing. He taught them what to eat. He taught them how to live long, healthy lives."

"And then?" I asked.

"He died," Dr. J replied. "Everybody dies … sooner or later."

"Awwh," Josh said.

"Did you know that Clara Barton worked here?" Dr. J asked.

"Clara who?"

"Clara Barton. She set up the Red Cross, and then she came to work here. In this building. Maybe right where we are now."

He acted like this was really special. And maybe it was. I think we talked about Clara Barton in history last year.

"So you *do* know history," I said.

"Yes," Dr. J replied. "And I also know about mice."

"Mice?" my brother asked.

"Yes, indeed," Dr. J replied. "Would you two boys like to see my mice?"

CHAPTER 4

No One Must Know

Personally, I don't like mice. We get mice in our house all the time. Mom screams when she sees them. Dad tries to hit them with a broom … and then he breaks stuff. Mice make trouble, if you ask me.

But my brother? He thinks mice are better than dogs!

So we followed Dr. J down the stairs, then back to a room at the east end of the hotel.

Dr. J opened the door and we saw a pretty nice

room. There was a bed, an old-fashioned couch, a nice carpet on the floor. Even glass in the window. But that wasn't the most amazing thing. The most amazing thing was on the floor.

There were mice.

Not a couple of mice. No. Not a dozen mice in a cage. No.

We saw a couple of hundred mice, all running around the floor. There were white mice, gray mice, pink mice (I swear!). They all looked up at Dr. J when he opened the door. They were like dogs waiting for table scraps.

"Sorry, children," Dr. J told them. "No goodies today."

I was feeling pretty creeped out. There were all these mice down by my feet. There was a crazy guy standing beside us. And my brother was acting as if this were all normal.

"I try to feed them," Dr. J told us. "I often get scraps from the dumpsters in town. But today ... well, I didn't feel very well today. Some days I feel more like a ghost than other days."

"Dr. J," I asked, "how long have you been here."

"Time!" he sighed. "Why do we care so much about time? We have the time we have, that's all. We have time enough, but never enough time. It is the tragedy of life." He lifted one hand to his head, like this was a great speech or something.

"Yeah, but how long have you been here?" Josh asked.

Dr. J looked up at my brother. "Maybe two months. I don't keep count."

"And how come you pretended to be a ghost?"

"Did I do that?"

"Yes!" Josh yelled. "And Kyle was scared."

"No I wasn't," I shot back.

"Yes you were. You peed your pants."

That shut me up pretty quick.

"Let me answer the question," Dr. J came in. "I acted like a ghost because sometimes I feel like a ghost. And ghosts keep people away. History shows us that some people take delight in hurting others. And I, myself, have come across many bad people. It is sad, but true."

"My teacher says there are no bad people," Josh replied. "Only people we don't understand."

"Is that so?" Dr. J asked. "And what grade are you in?"

"Grade 3."

"Perhaps by grade 4 you will learn otherwise," Dr. J told him. "History ... history suggests otherwise. I think your brother agrees with me."

27

Dr. J looked down at me.

"Well, I'm not sure," I said.

"You will learn. Pain is life's way of teaching us. Have you heard that before?"

"No."

"A man named George Bernard Shaw wrote that," Dr. J told us. "And it's true. I have learned – by pain – that some people are not nice. Some people want to hurt me. They'd even hurt a ghost." He stopped for a second, thinking back.

"But you're not a ghost," Josh said.

Dr. J just winked at me. He seemed so pale that he really did look like a ghost.

"Regardless, you two boys must keep the secret," he said.

"What secret?"

"Me," Dr. J told us. "If people find out that I'm here, there will be trouble. Teenagers are the worst. They love trouble. So you must tell no one about me."

We were quiet.

"Promise me?"

Both Josh and I nodded our heads.

"No one must know. Not your parents. Not your best friends. No one."

We nodded our heads.

"Thank you," Dr. J told us. "Now when you come to visit tomorrow, could you bring some cheese for the mice? They're hungry."

"What about you?" I asked.

"Oh, I never get hungry," Dr. J told me. "Never."

CHAPTER 5

Keeping the Secret

Josh and I were good. We kept Dr. J a secret. Each night we'd grab some food from the house and then take it up to the old hotel. I used some money I'd saved to buy cheese for the mice. I even learned the names of the mice: Rosie, Charlie, Marcie, Gus ... and a couple of hundred more.

Dr. J told us stories. They were history stories, so they were all about a long time ago. He told us about the Civil War. He told us how soldiers really died. (It's gross.) He told us about Clara Barton and the Red Cross. He told us how Dansville got its name. He even told us what *our* names meant. (Kyle means the water that lies between two islands. And Josh is from the Bible, short for Joshua.) Now is that cool, or what?

The only thing that bugged me was the "ghost" part. Was Dr. J a ghost or not? When Josh asked, Dr. J made a scary face. When I asked, Dr. J just winked. Sometimes he seemed pretty real. And sometimes – I swear – I could see right through him. It was weird.

That week, our mom was working afternoons at the hospital. She never asked where we went to play. She'd go mental if we told her about Dr. J at the Ghost Hotel. But Mom was too busy.

So every night, we learned about history and fed the mice. It was as simple as that. Maybe Dr. J was a ghost. Maybe he was a homeless guy. Maybe he was a professor. Who knew?

And we did keep the secret. Nobody would ever have found out about Dr. J … except I made a little mistake.

It was recess at school. I was out in the field when this big guy, Bruce Volat, came up to me. He didn't look real friendly.

"Hey, kid," he said. "How come you and your brother go sneaking up to the old hotel?"

"Me?" I replied. "Must be somebody else. You must be confused."

You should never tell a bully that he must be confused. It gets you a punch in the face.

So I got a punch in the face. When I got up, there was blood running from my nose.

"I asked you a question," Bruce said.

"I ... uh ..."

"How come you go up there? You and your brother. You always bring a bag of something. We seen you," he said.

I could have fixed his grammar. Bruce should have said, "We saw you." But I had a hunch that he'd just punch me in the face again.

"So?"

"There's a guy up there," I said. "We bring him food."

"What kind of guy? A bum? A homeless guy?"

"No, a professor."

From the look on his face, I don't think Bruce knew the word.

"Like a teacher," I added. And that seemed to go click in Bruce's brain.

"Okay," he said. His breath was pretty bad in my face. "The guys wanted to know."

"It's a secret," I said.

Bruce just laughed.

*　*　*

Dansville is a small town. Back a hundred years ago, Dr. J says we had 7000 people. Now we have about 1500. And news moves pretty fast in a small town.

The next day, my buddy Jake asked who was up in the old hotel. "The Ghost Hotel" is what he said. And I told him I didn't know.

And the day after that, all the kids were talking about the hotel. There was a homeless guy in the

Ghost Hotel. A bunch of robbers. Frankenstein!

Then my mom got in on it.

"Where do you two go play after dinner?"

"Next door," I lied.

"You don't like the kids next door," she said.

"Okay, down the street. There's a new kid."

"What's his name?"

"Franklin," I lied.

"A kid named Franklin?" my mother asked. She raised one eyebrow. She did that when she thought we were lying.

"Yeah, his mom named him after the turtle. Franklin the turtle."

That kind of shut my mother up. What could she say about some kid named after a turtle, even if he was a made-up kid?

"So have you heard about the homeless guy up in the old hotel?" my mom asked.

"What homeless guy?" we lied.

"A guy. Maybe a crazy guy," she said. "He could be dangerous, that's what I heard. The police went up to look for him."

I felt a kind of thunk in my stomach. Cops? Did the cops find Dr. J?

"Did they … uh …"

"No, nothing. Just a lot of mice. Somebody is feeding mice up there," mom said.

"Very strange," my brother told her. "Why would anyone feed rodents?"

Josh actually said that. He's been picking up words from the Professor. Josh learned that mice are rodents. Then he started looking up mice on the Internet. Mice are cool, Josh tells me.

So our mom let us off the hook. We got a warning, of course. "Don't you ever go playing up at the old hotel … or I'll ground you for the rest of your life."

And I didn't even say anything back.

But Josh was mad. That night, when we went to bed, he threw a pillow at me.

"You told," he said.

"I didn't," I lied.

"Yes you did," Josh replied. "Nobody knows about Dr. J but you and me. And I kept my mouth shut. So it had to be you."

My face was burning red. But the room was dark so Josh couldn't see. "Bruce Volat was beating me up," I admitted. "He made me tell."

"You're an idiot, Kyle."

"I ... uh ..."

"There are bad people, you know. There are people who will hurt Dr. J just for the fun of it."

"I thought ..."

Josh cut me off. "And if he gets hurt, it's because you can't keep a secret."

CHAPTER 6

A Warning

So the next night, after dinner, we went right to the Ghost Hotel. We didn't bring food for the mice. We didn't even bring food for Dr. J. We brought him a warning.

"Dr. J!" I called out.

"Professor!" my brother shouted.

Silence. We could both hear water dripping somewhere in the building. We could hear the mice – maybe – running along the floors. But mostly it was quiet.

"Is he still here?" I asked out loud.

"Maybe he left after the cops showed up," Josh suggested.

So we called out again, then waited. There was no sound for the longest time, and then we heard something weird.

"Whooooo?" came the sound. It sounded like the sound made an echo through the whole hotel. Then it came again. "Whooooo?"

"It's us," said my brother. That wasn't very intelligent, but it was true.

"Whoooo told the police?" came the voice. "Whooooo?"

"It was Kyle!" Josh shouted. "He told Bruce Volat, and Bruce told everybody in town. Kyle messed up big time."

We heard the sound of doors opening and closing. Then there were footsteps. And then Dr. J appeared at the top of the steps. He was dressed in that same white lab coat, but there seemed to be something different about him. For a second, I thought he was floating in the air.

"Good," Dr. J replied, "at least I know what happened."

"You're not mad?" Josh asked. "It's all because Kyle is an idiot."

Dr. J chose to ignore the second part of that. "No, I'm not mad," Dr. J told us as he came down the stairs. "It had to happen. Sooner or later, people would have to find out that I'm here. As Shakespeare said, 'Truth will out.'"

"Who?" Josh asked.

"Shakespeare," I said, hitting him with my elbow. "Don't they teach you anything in third grade?"

"Oh, yeah. Shakespeare," Josh replied. "That guy."

Both Dr. J and I looked at him. Josh just gave us a funny smile.

"I'm sorry," I said to Dr. J. "I guess I let the secret slip."

"Don't blame yourself, Kyle," the old professor replied. "Secrets only last so long. And ghosts don't scare everybody."

"How'd you make that scary voice?" Kyle asked.

"It's an old ear trumpet," Dr. J replied. "Before there were hearing aids, people would use an ear trumpet. If you talk into the small end, your voice comes out very loud."

"That's cool," Josh told him.

"Unfortunately, it is very hard to scare the police," Dr. J went on.

"Did they search all over?"

"Yes, but the police didn't find me," Dr. J told us. "Nor have any of your friends from school. They keep breaking in and looking around. Some nights, this place feels more like a real hotel than a Ghost Hotel. It's hard to get a good night's sleep."

Dr. J had a goofy smile on his face. It was as if Bruce Volat and the police were some kind of joke.

"We think that those teenagers could come back," I told Dr. J. "They're talking about Halloween. They might do something on Halloween."

"Is that coming up soon?" Dr. J asked me. "I'm afraid I don't have a calendar. And I left my day planner on a train someplace, so I'm not good with dates."

"Halloween is Friday," I said.

"Ah, that explains the cool weather."

"But that's when they're going to come," Josh broke in. "The teenagers could hurt you. They could kill you. They could do ANYTHING!" And then he started to cry.

Dr. J and I both looked at my brother. He was only eight years old, and sometimes it showed.

With tears running down his cheeks, he looked like he was five.

"Maybe I can scare them off with my ear trumpet," Dr. J told him.

Josh kept crying.

"Maybe they won't find me," he went on. "The police couldn't find me, even in the middle of the day."

Josh was still crying. I knew my brother – he could keep crying for a long time.

"Josh, cut it out," I told him. "I've got an idea about what we can do."

CHAPTER 7

Getting Ready

We had a few problems. There were only four days until Halloween, so that was a problem. We didn't have much money, so that was a problem. And I had to work with my brother – who is always a problem.

But we did come up with a pretty good plan.

All around school, the word was out. Bruce Volat and his gang were going to "take out" the homeless guy. They were going to "clean up" the Ghost Hotel. Bruce's gang wasn't that large –

44

maybe six guys. But it seemed like every other kid in high school might show up, too. That could be a crowd of a hundred teenagers! It could be like those old Frankenstein movies.

But we had some good luck, too. My brother had some money hidden away. It was only $23 in a piggy bank, but it was a start. Then I wrote a note that said it was okay to sell Josh fireworks. I signed my mom's name, and we were ready.

We both went down to the store that sold Halloween stuff. Then I sent my brother in alone. He's kind of cute, and he's only eight, so the old lady who ran the place gave him great deals. He came out with fake spiderwebs, plastic heads and phony blood. Then there was a whole box of fireworks. The kid got sparklers, cherry bombs and firecrackers. And then the grand prize – three Roman candles.

"Did I do good?" he asked me.

"You did great," I told him.

Of course, Josh didn't do all the work. I made up a plan of the house and where we could put stuff.

Then I went up to the hospital where mom works. I came back with a whole box of plastic gloves. A little sand in those, a little fake blood, and we had a bunch of scary dead hands. Then I went to the basement and came up with an old record player. The old kind – way before CDs. The thing ran on batteries, so I bought some D cells. With a couple of old records, the thing was screeching like a ghost.

That night, we went up to show Dr. J. But he wasn't impressed.

"Why go to all this trouble?" he said. "Maybe it's time for me to move on."

"Move on!" I said. "Are you going to let a stupid gang chase you away? Are you going to give in to bullies?" I was almost shouting. "No, you are not!" I answered my own questions. "You're going to stand and fight!"

"Fight?" Dr. J asked.

"Okay, so stand and scare them off," I explained. "Here's what we'll do."

So I pulled out my plan. I showed him how it would all work, step by step. It was a pretty good plan, even if only half of it worked. But Dr. J was still having trouble.

"What if it doesn't work?" he asked. "Then those teenagers will be angry as well as stupid. What then?"

"Then I have a secret back-up plan," I said.

Both Josh and Dr. J looked at me with big eyes.

"Which is what?" Josh asked.

"I'm not going to tell you," I said. "If I did, it wouldn't be secret. Would it?"

That stopped them both. I mean, what could anybody say to that?

The next night, we started work on the non-secret plan. We put up spider webs and hid the stuffed gloves. We ran string to the doors. We tested the old record player. We got the fireworks ready to go. Then we aimed the Roman candles.

It was perfect. From the third-floor hall, we could scare anybody who might be down on the first floor. If it all worked, Bruce Volat would be peeing his pants on Halloween night. If not, I still had my secret weapon.

CHAPTER 8

Halloween

On Halloween, Josh and I got dressed up for tricks and treats. Josh was a ghost and I was a ghoul. We told Mom we were going out with Franklin. Then we'd be hanging out at Franklin's house. Mom just sighed and told us to be careful.

"There's a homeless guy up at the old hotel, you know," she said. "He could be dangerous."

"Oh Mom," we replied. "Take it easy."

By seven o'clock, we got up to the Ghost Hotel.

Out front, there were already some teenagers hanging around, so Josh and I had to sneak in the back way. None of the teenagers had come inside yet. They must be waiting for Bruce to show up. We tried to be really quiet as we went upstairs.

"Do you see them?" Dr. J whispered to us. He looked even whiter than usual – like a piece of tracing paper. "Those teenagers look very mean. Very, very mean."

"Don't be scared," I said. "They're just teenagers. That means they're kind of stupid. If we can get one guy running and screaming, they'll all panic."

"Are you sure?" Josh asked.

"Sure I'm sure," I told him. And I tried to act like I meant it. I still had my secret back-up plan, but I hoped we wouldn't need it.

For an hour, we waited. More and more teenagers gathered outside. I counted about fifty of them. And that was even before Bruce and his gang showed up. There was a lot of shouting and cursing. Some of them were drinking – and not just Coke.

"We could call the police," Josh suggested.

"On Halloween?" I replied. "What are they going to do, anyhow?"

"Maybe arrest them," Josh answered. "Like for underage drinking."

"Yeah, right," I replied. "I say we stick with the plan."

There really was no time to call the cops, or anybody. In five minutes, the gang began moving up the big entry stairs. Soon they had pushed open the doors and moved into the grand ballroom.

Then we heard Bruce Volat shout out, "Oh Bum! Oh Freak! Where are you?" There was a pause. A bunch of the other kids laughed. "You've got company!"

"You can still run out of here," Dr. J whispered.

"Shhh!" I whispered back.

"We're coming to get you …" Bruce said, and then he laughed.

It was time for the plan. Now or never.

"Start the music," I whispered to Josh.

Soon the old scratchy record began to play. It sounded really spooky.

"Push those buttons," I whispered to Dr. J.

A bunch of old flashguns went off. *Pop, pop, pop.* Each one gave a big flash of light. Then it was dark again.

We heard talking downstairs.

"I can't see," said one teenager.

"This is too weird for me," said another.

"Maybe this place really is haunted," said a third.

It was time to bring out more noise. I told Josh to light a string of firecrackers, then throw them downstairs.

Pop-pop-poppa-pop-pop-poppa-pop-pop- poppa-pop-pop.

"Pull the strings," I whispered to Dr. J.

In a second, five doors began to slam. One pull to slam, a little slack on the string, and then a second slam.

And then, our best number – the Roman candles. Roman candles are the coolest kind of fireworks.

"Fire number one," I told Josh.

"Aye, aye, captain," he said. I think he had the

wrong kind of movie in mind, but so what?

The lighter set off our first Roman candle. We had aimed it down the central hall, and it flew perfectly. *Zoom*. Then it exploded just as the teenagers were coming up the stairs.

"That could have killed me," one guy shouted.

"I'm getting out of here," another guy said.

Soon the second guy was pushing back down the stairs. There seemed to be a lot of panic down in the ballroom. A bunch of teenagers had already run out the door.

Then a girl came running from another room.

"A dead body!" she shrieked. "There's a dead body in there!"

It was not, really, a dead body. But it was a dead-looking plastic glove filled with sand. The fingers were red from fake blood.

"I found somebody's arm!" shrieked another kid. "I'm gonna puke!"

And then he did. What a mess!

It was getting pretty wild. I was afraid some of the teenagers would get hurt in the stampede to get out. They were screaming and pushing, shoving and running. It was panic, sheer panic.

"Nice job, Kyle," my brother said.

"We're not done yet," I told him.

Bruce Volat was still downstairs, and three of his guys were still with him.

Bruce raised a fist and looked upstairs. "You can't scare us, Freak!"

CHAPTER 9

Yes We Can

It was a standoff. Bruce was downstairs, looking up. We were upstairs, looking down.

Bruce and his gang were angry. They'd been made to look like idiots. And we were scared because they hadn't run off.

"BRUUUCE, GO HOME," I said through the ear trumpet.

Bruce and his friends just laughed. Our bag of scary tricks was running low. Now it was four teenagers against two kids and one old guy.

Lousy odds.

"They're not scared," my brother whispered.

"I can see that," I whispered back.

"Maybe you can sneak past them," Dr. J whined. "I'll be all right. Really I will."

"Shhh!" I said. "It's time for the secret weapon."

Bruce and his gang were coming up the stairs. Thump-thump-thump. They were in no hurry. They didn't know where we were. And they didn't know what else we might have.

"Slam the doors one more time," I whispered to Dr. J. I figured that would slow them down. They'd have to go check all the rooms on the second floor. "And get the next Roman candle ready. In five seconds, light it. That should give me some time."

So the doors began to slam. And then the rocket went shooting down, exploding into a hundred little sparks.

I didn't have time to admire the fireworks. I had to use our last hope.

"We're going to find you, Freak," Bruce shouted up. "You can't scare us with noises and fireworks.

And you can't hide all night."

They were checking out the rooms on the second floor. One by one, the strings broke. The doors stopped slamming. And the gang got closer.

"We're coming upstairs, Freak. We know you're up there."

By then I was back with Josh and Dr. J. I could see Bruce and his gang coming up the stairs. They weren't far away.

It was time for the secret weapon.

"What's that?" Josh asked as I brought it in.

"A cat box," I said.

"Is that the secret weapon?" Dr. J asked. His eyes were wide with terror. I really think he was afraid.

"No," I said. "The cat sets off the weapon. Let's move."

Bruce and his gang reached the top of the metal stairs. We ran down the hall.

"Sounds like there's more than one freak," said one voice.

"We can handle 'em," Bruce replied. Then he let out a sick, sick laugh. I could hear him smashing

one fist into his palm.

Time was running out. We raced back to the last of the third-floor rooms. It was the room where Dr. J fed the mice. In fact, it was a room filled with hundreds and hundreds of mice. Most of the time, the mice had no reason to go anywhere. They sat around waiting for Dr. J to bring food.

But today, I brought them a cat!

I threw the cat back into one corner. He gave a

nasty growl and chased the nearest mouse. That poor guy was a goner.

But the other mice got the message. They ran! They darted and dashed along the floor. They scrurried as fast as any mice have ever scurried.

Soon there was a tidal wave of mice pouring out the door … and down the hall … and right at Bruce Volat and his gang!

"Ohmygod!" they screamed. "Rats. He's sending rats!"

Actually, they were mice. But I saw no reason to tell them.

"They're climbing on me!" cried one guy. "Let me out of here!"

"I've got one in my hair. Ohmygod! It's biting me!"

Soon Bruce and his gang were running down the stairs. It was more than panic. This time it was real fear. They weren't afraid of us that much, but rats! Now that was something else.

"That was amazing," Josh said. He looked at me with big eyes. It was as if he finally knew just how smart I was.

"Thank you," I replied. "One of my better ideas, I'd say."

And I thought it really was a very good idea. It certainly stopped Bruce and his gang. I was grinning in triumph.

The only problem was Dr. J. He was crying, really crying.

"My little friends," Dr. J wailed. "They're gone."

CHAPTER 10

A Letter

The next night, we came up after supper – just like always. We even brought some cheese for the mice. After all the work they'd done, the mice deserved a reward.

But the Ghost Hotel had changed. It felt colder and darker than before. When we called out for Dr. J, there was an echo. It was as if nobody was there. It was as if nobody had ever been there.

So we took the back stairs up to the third floor.

"Dr. J!" I called out. But there was no answer.

"Professor!" my brother yelled. But there was no answer.

We walked down the hall to the mouse room. That's where Dr. J kept all the mice. And they had to be hungry after chasing Bruce and his gang.

But when we opened the door, there were no mice. There was no furniture. There was nothing at all.

"What happened?" Josh asked.

"It's all gone," I said. I felt a shiver go up and down my spine. "The couch, the carpet, the mice. It's like nothing was here."

"But it was," Josh said. "We saw it."

"We saw something," I told him. "Something," I repeated.

We walked up the stairs to the top floor. There was a little moonlight coming through the old roof. It was just enough light to see an envelope stuck to the wall.

"It's for us," Josh said, pulling it off.

"This is very strange," I told my brother. "Very weird."

It was too dark to read the letter in the hotel, so we brought it home. My mom was surprised to see us come in so early. She was *very* surprised when we said we had to go study.

We didn't study our school books. What we studied was the letter.

Dear Kyle and Josh,

I am sorry there was no time to say goodbye. I much enjoyed meeting both of you. And I have to thank you for scaring away those teenagers. They would have made staying here very difficult.

But I just got a job offer: I have a new job teaching history in New York City. I had to take the first train this morning to get there in time. So I must leave you with my best wishes. As we say in Latin, vale, vale. *Go well and be well, my young friends.*

Best regards, from your friend and teacher,
Dr. James C. Jackson

Of course, Josh began to cry. I felt kind of sad, too. I wondered if there really was a job in New York. I wondered if my scaring the mice was behind it. I wondered about a lot of things.

But one thing I knew for sure. There was no train to New York. There hadn't been a train to New York for fifty years ... or more.

Two Years Later

So Dr. J was out of our lives. We heard nothing from him. The Ghost Hotel stayed empty. There were no strange lights at night. Life became kind of dull.

But then my brother came running in from school one day. He was in grade 5 by then. His class was studying local history. And Josh had a book in his hand: *Around Dansville*.

"Look, look," he panted, out of breath.

"What?"

"The picture," he panted. "A real old picture. Look!"

So I opened the book to the page he had marked. It was just one page in a whole chapter on Dr. Jackson's Sanatorium.

And there was a photograph, dated 1892. It showed Clara Barton, a couple of other people and Dr. James C. Jackson in a white lab coat.

"It's him!" Josh cried. "It's the professor."

I stared at the old picture for the longest time. I kept telling myself that it was impossible. Dr. Jackson died seventy years ago. There's no such thing as ghosts. It just wasn't possible.

But I couldn't get over the picture. The face, the eyes, the lab coat. I knew the man in the picture.

"It's him, isn't it?" Josh demanded.

I nodded. For once, my brother was absolutely right.